HUMPHREY'S BEAR

By Jan Wahl · Illustrated by William Joyce

HENRY HOLT AND COMPANY   NEW YORK

Published by Henry Holt and Company, Inc.,
115 West 18th Street, New York, New York 10011.
Published in Canada by Fitzhenry & Whiteside Limited,
195 Allstate Parkway, Markham, Ontario L3R 4T8.

Library of Congress Cataloging in Publication Data
Wahl, Jan.
Humphrey's Bear.
Summary: Humphrey has wonderful adventures with his
toy bear after they go to bed at night, just as his
father did before him.
1. Children's stories, American. [1. Bedtime—
Fiction.   2. Bears—Fiction]   I. Joyce, William, ill.
II. Title.
PZ7.W1266Hu   1987   [E]   85-5541
ISBN: 0-8050-0332-0

Printed in Italy
3   5   7   9   10   8   6   4   2

ISBN 0-8050-0332-0

For Elizabeth Upham McWebb,
who lives in the bear house

—J.W.

For my lifelong pal
and confidante, Melissa

—W. J.

When Humphrey went up the stairs to bed he heard his father say—

"Isn't Humphrey too old to sleep with a toy bear?"

Humphrey didn't hear what his mom said.

He just jumped under the blanket and snuggled with the brown bear and slept.

The bear was very old. It had been Humphrey's father's bear long ago.

As soon as Humphrey was asleep, the bear grew as big as it always did and took him by the hand.

"Get up!" called the big bear, standing in the moonlight. "Our boat is waiting."

"Here is your cap. Get moving!"

Sleepy, Humphrey followed downstairs and out the kitchen door, quietly—so that his parents didn't hear him.

There was a river running beyond the wet, green night grass and at the end of long planks lay a sailboat.

"Take the helm. Steer!" shouted the bear, pulling the ropes of high-flying sails. "Cast off!"

They sailed right out of the backyard.

A nice wind whooshed them along, and after a while the bear served Humphrey and himself a cup of hot chocolate.

Pretty soon the river flowed into a
huge wet sea, and porpoises sang sea songs
for them.

Humphrey steered by the stars, while the
shaggy bear with a banjo danced a fine jig.

Suddenly, a typhoon came up out of nowhere

and the bear slipped and fell off the deck.

Humphrey dived for his friend.

"Where are you?" said Humphrey.

"Blub blub!" said the bear.

"I will *save* you!" yelled Humphrey. However he could not find the bear, though he swam and he swam and he swam . . .

. . . until he came to an island.

Over a sandly hill he heard a dreamy banjo playing.

Seashells pinched his feet as
Humphrey climbed the sandy hill.

He found the bear, and the warm
moon outside and hot chocolate
inside dried them.

Humphrey could smell the bear's wonderful furry fur.

They shut their eyes and the next thing Humphrey knew . . .

. . . he was in his bed.

"*Bear! Where ARE you?*" yelled Humphrey.

His father was holding the toy bear in the moonlight. His father was remembering when that bear was *his* bear.

"Here, Son," whispered his father.

His mom stood in the half-opened door, smiling, as his father put the little bear back in Humphrey's hands.

"I used to sail with him, too."